THE WORLD'S
WINDIEST BABY

Steve Hartley is a sensible man. He has a sensible job, a sensible family, lives in a sensible house and drives a sensible car. But underneath it all, he longs to be silly. There have been occasional forays into silliness: Steve has been a football mascot called Desmond Dragon, and has tasted World Record success himself – taking part in both a mass yodel and a mass yo-yo. But he wanted more, and so his alter ego – Danny Baker Record Breaker – was created. Steve lives in Lancashire with his wife and teenage daughter.

You can find out more about Steve
on his extremely silly website:
www.stevehartley.net

STEVE HARTLEY

THE WORLD'S
WINDIEST BABY

ILLUSTRATED BY KATE PANKHURST

MACMILLAN CHILDREN'S BOOKS

First published 2011 by Macmillan Children's Books
a division of Macmillan Publishers Limited
20 New Wharf Road, London N1 9RR
Basingstoke and Oxford
Associated companies throughout the world
www.panmacmillan.com

ISBN 978-0-330-53372-0

3 5 7 9 8 6 4

A CIP catalogue record for this book is available from
the British Library.

Printed and bound in the UK by CPI Group (UK) Ltd, Croydon, CR0 4YY

For Rosie

This is entirely a work of fiction and any resemblance
to the real world is purely coincidental.

On the
Scrapheap

WARNING!
This story
is rubbish!

Yawn!

To the Keeper of the Records
The Great Big Book of World Records
London

Dear Mr Bibby

Yesterday we had a mega-
boring lesson about how
paint dries, and halfway
through it I did a massive

Bogey Balls

yawn! I was really tired because I'd been up
late rolling my bogey balls, getting them ready
for the County Bogey-flicking Championships next
month.

The yawn was a jaw buster!
It spread through the class
and in seconds everyone in
the room was yawning too.

YAWN!

To make things worse, we had a Nuffsed inspector sitting in on the lesson. He was right next to me, so there was no way he could escape the yawn!

I couldn't stop and did about ten in a row! Our teacher, Mrs Woodcock, was just about to tell me off when SHE yawned too.

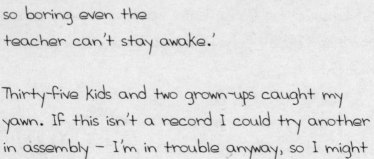

I saw the Nuffsed Inspector write in his book, 'The lessons are so boring even the teacher can't stay awake.'

Thirty-five kids and two grown-ups caught my yawn. If this isn't a record I could try another in assembly — I'm in trouble anyway, so I might as well give it a go!

Best wishes
Danny Baker

PS I've got to collect all the litter around school as a punishment. The Penleydale bin men are on strike, and rubbish is building up everywhere.

PPS The Nuffsed inspector gave our school an official rating of Outstandingly Boring!

Dear Danny

Unfortunately, unless you have 53,209 people
in your school assembly, there's no point in
attempting the Most Infectious Yawn world
record. It happened in 2009 during the second
half of a World Cup qualifying football
match between Mulldovia and Bulldozia. A draw
meant that both teams would go through, so
neither tried to score – they simply passed the
ball around in the centre of the pitch. After
seventy-one minutes the Mulldovia manager,
Fibbio Caputti, was so bored that he did an
enormous yawn. At that very moment his face
was on the two big screens at either end of the
stadium and in 25.33 seconds everyone – players,
spectators, substitutes and the referee – was
yawning too!

As a matter of interest, the Most Boring Lesson
Ever Taught took place on 3 October 1988 in
the aptly named town of Boring, in Oregon, USA.
During a long algebra lesson, teacher Libby
Bangasser sent her entire class of thirty-seven
children to sleep. Eight of the children were
snoozing so deeply they couldn't be woken for
over thirteen hours! Her numeracy lessons have
been recorded, and are now prescribed by doctors
as a cure for insomnia.

Best wishes
Eric Bibby
Keeper of the Records

'What's a *Pamper Party*?' asked Danny as a stream of his mum's friends bustled noisily into the house.

'It's a girlie-thing,' replied Mum. 'We try on make-up and perfume, and a lady from the Pom-Pom Pamper Parlour will make us all look beautiful.'

Danny frowned and stared at his sister. 'What, even Nat? They'll need a truck full of make-up to do that!'

Natalie peered down her nose at her brother as though he was something green and slimy that had crawled out of a swamp. 'Even a tanker full of perfume wouldn't make you and your stinky baby brother smell better.'

'Why don't me and Matt stay and organize some party games for you?' suggested Danny. 'We could all play musical trumps while your nail varnish is drying.'

'This is a girls-only party,' said Dad, guiding the

boys towards the front door. 'We're going to have a boys-only trip to the Great Goalton Home for Abandoned Football Mascots.'

'Ace!' said Danny.

'Cool!' agreed Matthew.

Half an hour later, Dad turned down a narrow country lane and the car bumped and bounced along the rough road until they reached an enormous pair of rusty iron gates. The sign above the gates was lopsided and had letters missing.

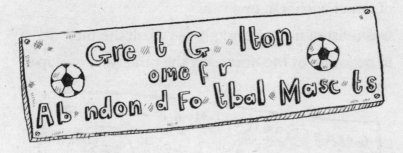

Behind the desk in the ticket office stood a giant pork chop, wearing the blue and white colours of Queen's Pork Rovers. He had a face with a wide toothy smile and one eye closed in a permanent wink.

'Hi kids!' he called, giving them the thumbs-up as they came through the door. 'Welcome to Goalton! I'm Choppy the Chop!'

The chop rummaged beneath the ticket desk and handed the boys a sheet of paper each. On one side was a list of names and photos of all the mascots to be found at the home; on the other was a map

of Great Goalton, with the timings for various activities and demonstrations. The place was set out like a village, with buildings arranged around a central village green: a plastic Cosmograss five-a-side pitch, where most of the fun seemed to take place. There was a museum, a cafe, souvenir shops and ice-cream stands. Dotted around the site were 'Meet the Mascot' dugouts, where autographs could be signed and photographs taken.

While Choppy the Chop signed Matthew's sheet, Danny studied the mascot list.

Spot the Mascot!

How many autographs can YOU *collect?*

Bladderpool: Billy Bladder, sponsored by Glenlouie Toilet Paper Company Ltd
Downmouth Albion: Poppy the Pimple, sponsored by Dollop's Spot and Boil Cream

Hartleypuddle United: Willy Welly, sponsored by Drip-dry Wellingtons

Neverton: Percy Pants, sponsored by Wigglesworth's Y-fronts Ltd

 Nitts County: Nat the Nit, sponsored by Fleas-R-Gone

Nuttingham Shrubbery: Samson Spade, sponsored by the Bloomin' Great Garden Centre

 Queen's Pork Rovers: Choppy the Chop, sponsored by Bobbett's Butchers

Sheepfield Thursday: Baa- Baa the Blacksheep, sponsored by the Great Balls of Wool knitting shop

 Totterton Hotspoons: Totty Teaspoon, sponsored by Tiddley's Teabags

Towchester Town: Stubby the Toe, sponsored by Fung-away Foot Powder

Tubbercurry Poppadoms: Pippa Poppadom, sponsored by Tandoor Takeaways

Uddersfield Town: Moo-Moo La
 Moor, sponsored by Dangleby
 Dairies

Walchester United: Wally the Wall,
 sponsored by Knock 'Em Down
 Demolition Ltd

Wimpleton: Wendy Wimple, sponsored by
 Hatty Horton's House of Hats

They began their visit in the little museum just
behind the ticket office by watching the *Mascot
Memories* film: 'Twenty minutes of mascot magic
and mayhem through the years'. Danny especially
liked the part in 1968 when Belgian Bobby (a huge
walnut-whip chocolate) was late for a friendly
game between Belgium and Lichtenstein and, in his
rush to get on to the pitch, forgot to put the lower
half of his suit on before he ran out.

'From then on,' said the voiceover the film. 'He
was known as Belgian Botty!'

Next Danny, Matthew and Dad hurried along
to the pitch in the centre of the village to join in

the *Groovy Goal Celebrations*
show. During the demonstration,
Stubby the Toe taught them how to moonwalk
while wearing huge plastic football boots.

The moment the show was over, the boys raced
to the Offside Souvenir shop, then over to the
Vintage Shirts and Shorts shop, stopping on the
way to collect autographs at the covered Meet the
Mascot dugouts nearby.

Danny noticed that, like the sign at the entrance,
everything in Great Goalton was shabby, worn and
broken. Weeds grew from cracks in the footpaths,
and the paint on doors and window frames was
peeling away. There were actually more mascots

than visitors. Only six people turned up for the
Classic Football Chants show, and although Wendy
Wimple urged the audience to 'sing and shout your
socks off', the sound echoed emptily around the
five-a-side pitch.

At lunchtime Dad took the boys to the
Cornerkick Cafe for pie and chips with mushy peas
and gravy. With full tummies, they returned to wait
for the five-a-side football match to start.

'Look, Dan!' said Matthew. 'There's Wally the
Wall!'

The ex-Walchester United mascot was sitting
glumly inside a Meet the Mascot dugout, the
name of his sponsors –
Knock 'Em Down
Demolition Ltd –
splashed in
white paint
across the
front of
his red
rubber

brick-wall suit. Wally had been replaced at the club by Wibbles the Dribbling Jelly when Wibberley Wobberley Jellies became the team's new sponsors.

'You don't want my autograph,' grumbled Wally as Danny and Matt posed with him for a photo. 'I'm just a wall with legs. I was given the push by a dribbling jelly.'

'Wibbles looks stupid,' said Danny.

'Yeah,' agreed Matthew. 'A wall's a much better mascot than a jelly.'

Wally the Wall perked up a little. 'Thanks, lads,' he said, signing the boys' Spot the Mascot sheets.

'I bet it's more fun being here than at Walchester,' said Dad.

'It is!' replied Wally. 'But the home's going to close at the end of the month. It's run by the council, and they promised to give us a million pounds, but instead the money's gone to build a new extension at the Toot Modern Art Gallery in Penleydale.' The mascot sighed. 'It won't be long before we're all thrown on the scrapheap – out of a job, *again*.'

'But this place is Ace!' cried Danny. 'It can't close!'

The rubber bricks of Wally's costume wobbled as he shrugged. 'You'd better go and watch the game while you still can,' he said.

Dad and the boys pushed through the rusty turnstiles once more and sat down on the cracked and splintered wooden benches running down one edge of the five-a-side pitch. Two teams of mascots jogged on to the patchy green plastic turf to the cheers of the very small crowd: Choppy's Champs wearing red bibs over their club shirts, and Totty's Tearaways in blue bibs.

The match was end to end. Choppy the Chop scored a hat-trick, including one from an overhead kick. Percy Pants made some fantastic sliding tackles, but Stubby the Toe stubbed his toe and was stretchered off by Moo-Moo La Moor and Baa-Baa the Blacksheep.

Just as the referee blew the final whistle, Billy Bladder scored with a fantastic diving header, and the game ended 4–4. It came down to a penalty shoot-out. Pippa Poppadom missed, and Poppy the

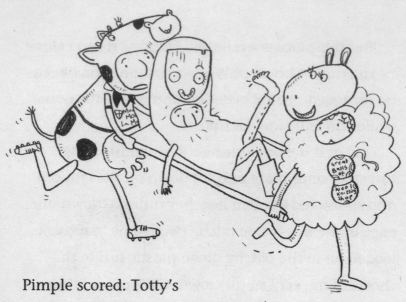

Pimple scored: Totty's
Tearaways had won the game.

The day finished with the March of the
Mascots – a parade around the arena accompanied
by the Great Goalton Vuvuzela Band. As Danny
listened to the horrible honking horns, he knew
what he had to do.

'This place *can't*
close,' said Danny.
'I've had an idea . . .'

'Uh-oh,' said Dad. 'I
don't like the sound of
this.'

'I'm going to raise a million pounds and save the mascots!' announced Danny. 'I'll ask people to sponsor me to break records!'

'Cool idea, Dan,' said Matthew.

Dad smiled and ruffled his son's hair. 'Good for you,' he said. 'I'll see if Walchester United will give you a hundred pounds to get your fund off the ground, in memory of Wally the Wall.'

Later that evening at home, Danny sat with his baby brother Joey on his knee, trying to teach him how to blow raspberries. He told Mum and Natalie about his Big Plan.

'I'll give you a pound to break the record for telling me how beautiful I look,' suggested his sister, gently patting her new hairstyle, and showing off her long pink fingernails.

Mum laughed. 'You've never done it before, Danny,' she said. 'Once will be enough to break *that* record!'

Pants

Dear Mr Bibby

I've started a Mascots in
Need appeal to stop the Great
Goalton Home for Abandoned
Football Mascots from closing
down. I've not got long – their
money runs out soon! I've
written to all their old sponsors, to see if they'll
make a donation for every record I attempt.

Wigglesworth's Y-Fronts in Neverton gave me £50
to try to break the record for wearing the
most underpants on my head, putting on one
pair over the top of another. I started with
small ones, moved up to medium sized as the
underpant hat grew bigger, large ones when it
got enormous, and extra large when it became

ginormous! Wigglesworth even gave me some extra-EXTRA-large super-elasticated pants to use when the helmet got mega-massive!

me, with pants on my head ↗

By the time I'd got forty-two pairs of pants on my head I had to give up because the hat was so heavy I kept falling over! I think I've got the world's stiffest neck now. I'm sending you a photo that Matt took — it looks Ace!

Have I broken the world record for the biggest underpant hat?

Best wishes
Danny Baker

Dear Danny

What a great idea and what a fantastic cause to raise money for.

Did you know that in the town of Neverton, where Wigglesworth's Y-Fronts are made, the people have a custom of wearing their pants on their heads on the first Sunday of every month, in honour of the factory's founder, Tommy 'Tiggle' Wigglesworth? He was so proud of his underpants that he not only wore them over his trousers, but also on his head. In the 1920s, posh French fashion designer Jean-Tour de France stole the idea and started a craze that saw high society ladies wearing fancy ballgowns with diamonds around their necks and underpants on their heads.

23

I'm afraid that your brave attempt at the Most Underpants Worn on a Single Head record fell quite a few pants short. The record is held by Denis Welch, one of Wigglesworth's Grade A gusset-stitchers, who in 1985 piled 636 pairs on his head, producing a helmet with a circumference of 193.7 cm, weighing 31.8 kg. The weight of the pant pile pushed Denis's head down into his shoulders, and he now looks like he's permanently shrugging.

Bad luck, Danny. I can't wait to see what other records you're going to try to break. I hope you have some generous donors!

Best wishes
Eric Bibby
Keeper of the Records

Danny and
Matthew had
been practising for an
hour in Penleydale Park
for their next sponsored
record attempt: Long-distance
Spoon-launched Used-teabag Propulsion
(teapot-hat target). Matthew stood ten
metres away from Danny with his grandma's
big brown china teapot tied to his head by string
fastened under his chin. Danny had a bucket at his
feet full of used Tiddley's teabags, which he had
rescued from the teachers' rubbish bin at school.

For the umpteenth time he carefully placed one
soggy teabag on the end of a teaspoon and, with
a quick flick of his wrist, sent it arcing towards
Matthew. The teabag sailed well over his friend's
head and into the grass a couple of metres behind
him. Danny tried again. This time the mushy
missile smacked with a damp slap on to Matt's
nose and stuck there, alongside the ones already
plastered on Matthew's right eye and chin.

'This is really hard,' said Danny.

'You're not the one covered in teabags!' Matthew reminded him.

Just then, Mrs Grimshaw, the park keeper, walked past them carrying four big plastic sacks full of rubbish. 'I hope you're going to pick up those teabags, young man,' she said. 'There's enough litter piling up in my park without you adding to it.'

'Don't worry,' replied Danny. 'We'll clear up.'

'This bin strike's ruining my flower-beds,' she grumbled. 'Who wants to come to the park when there are piles of rubbish lying around? I wish I knew someone who'd shift it – I'd pay them myself.'

'We'll take it away for you,' offered Danny.

'Would you?' said Mrs Grimshaw. 'You know, you two could earn yourselves some *real* pocket money. There're lots of people on the High Street struggling with their rubbish. Go and see Elsie at

Stubbins's Sticky Bun Shop – I know she'll give you
something to get rid of hers.'

'Ace! Thanks!' grinned Danny.

'What're *we* going to do with bags of rubbish?'
whispered Matt.

Danny shrugged. 'We'll find somewhere to put
them,' he said. 'And we can add the money to the
Mascots in Need appeal.'

But when Mrs Grimshaw dumped the bulging
black bin liners down in front of them, Danny
began to wonder if he'd been a bit hasty.

'Wow,' he gasped. 'They're . . . big!'

'Mega-big,' agreed Matthew.

Mrs Grimshaw gave them a pound each. 'There's
four more behind my office,' she said. 'There'll be
another pound for you when those are shifted
too.'

'Ace!' said Danny, heaving one bag of rubbish
on to his back and dragging the other behind him.
'We'll be back later!'

The boys lugged the heavy sacks through town,
looking for somewhere to put them. All the rubbish

bins were full to overflowing. Some shop owners had hired skips, but those were full too. Danny hadn't realized just how much rubbish had built up since the binmen had gone on strike.

'There's nowhere to put them,' he puffed as they staggered on to Tempest Road, past the Sports Centre and the Crumbly Crunch biscuit factory towards the art gallery. 'What're we going to do with them?'

'Why don't we hide them in your bedroom?' laughed Matthew. 'It's already a tip, so no one will notice.'

'Oh no!' cried Danny, staring behind him. The sack he was dragging along had ripped open, leaving along the pavement a trail of cold leftover fish and chips, mouldy flower heads, Bustagut burger boxes, snotty hankies, chewing gum and a plastic bag containing what looked like doggy doo-doo.

A mouse poked its head out of the hole in the sack. It hesitated before scurrying through a gap under the high wooden fence that ran along the

edge of the pavement.

Danny and Matthew stared at the fence that had been blocking the entrance to the Art Gallery for weeks.

'My dad said that they were building a new bit on to the art gallery,' said Matthew. 'But the work had to stop because all the bricklayers got Funnybone-itis of the Elbow.'

'Jimmy Sedgley says that's just a story to cover up the *real* truth,' said Danny. 'His cousin's best friend's older sister said that the builders dug so deep they went right to the centre of the earth and got frazzled by red-hot lava!'

Matthew shook his head. 'That's not what I heard,' he said. 'Josh Pettigrew said that his grandad knows a man who drives a digger, and *he* said they'd uncovered a black hole, and got sucked into another part of the universe!'

Danny began to collect the rubbish he'd left behind. 'So if we chuck these bags over the fence, they'll either get burnt to a crisp or disappear into space?'

Matthew nodded. 'And that'll solve the problem of where to put them!'

Danny shoved the spilt rubbish back into the bin bag, and hurled it over the fence.

The boys listened for the clunk as it hit the ground on the other side, but there was only silence.

Matthew threw one of his bags over.

Silence.

'It's true!' he gasped. 'They're falling to the centre of the earth!'

'Or into the black hole!' said Danny. 'Come on, let's get the rest from the park, then go and see Elsie Stubbins.'

The boys cleared the soggy sacks from around the back of the Sticky Bun Shop and the Eat Your Greens grocers next door. The gooey stink of sour cream, mouldy jam and stale cakes crawled out and mixed with the sickly sweet fug of putrefying potatoes, rotting raspberries and liquefying leeks.

'This pong's worse than my socks,' said Danny, throwing a sack of squishy satsumas and bad bananas over the fence.

'Where are you putting all this rubbish?' asked Elsie when the boys returned.

'We've found some space for it,' replied Danny.

'I've spread the word around all the other shops on the High Street,' she said, handing the boys a pound each. 'They'll give you some money if you move their binbags too.'

'I'm building a rubbish cart tonight,' said Matthew. 'We'll need it!'

'Ace!' said Danny. 'We're going to earn a fortune for the Mascots in Need appeal!'

Udder rubbish

Dear Mr Bibby

I think I've broken a record! Dangleby Dairies, who sponsor Moo-Moo La Moor, Uddersfield Town's old mascot, gave me £10 to go for the Long-distance Udder-milk Squirting record. They even let me borrow a cow — a champion Somerset Squirter called Saffron. She squirts for England!

Moo-Moo La Moor

Squeezing milk from a cow's udder is really hard. It took me ages to get it right, but then POW! I got it! Mutthew made a Squirting Range, with measurements on the floor, and my best squirt

udder

milk!

went 34.29 metres. But was it a record squirt?

Best wishes
Danny Baker

PS Me and Matt have raised £218.53 for
Mascots in Need. There's a long way to go, but
it's a good start!

The Great Big Book
of World Records
London

ARE YOU A RECORD
BREAKER ?

Dear Danny,

I'm sorry to have to tell you that your
fantastic Long-distance Udder Squirt isn't
a record. By an amazing coincidence, the day
before your letter arrived I received one from
Professor Oswaldo Bozzo, of the Venezuelan
Udder Research Laboratories in Caracas. He has
bred a cow called Delores, whose udders have
been genetically engineered to deliver a high-
powered spurt of milk. She gives more volume
in less time than even a champion Somerset
Squirter.

Last week, Manuela Delsoto, the Venezuelan
manual milking champion, was invited to have a
squeeze. Manuela and Delores produced a squirt
measuring a stupendous 56.99 metres. Delores's

35

stream of milk was so powerful that Manuela
was able to shoot cola cans off a wall from
thirty metres away.

Bad luck, Danny, but milking a cow is always a
useful skill to have — you never know when it
may come in handy!

Best wishes
Eric Bibby
Keeper of the Records

Danny walked stiffly into morning assembly at school. He couldn't bend his arms or legs, because Matthew had wrapped Danny's whole body in Glenlouie Soft and Silky toilet paper. He was wearing his school uniform underneath so that he wouldn't get into trouble.

Kids began to nudge each other and chuckle. The chuckling turned to giggling, then, as more children spotted him, into guffaws that echoed through the hall.

'Daniel Baker!' shouted 'Beaky' Rogers, the head teacher. 'What on *earth* are you playing at?'

'The Glenlouie Toilet Paper Company's sponsoring my record attempt for the longest time

dressed as a loo-paper mummy, sir,' replied
Danny.

Mr Rogers sighed and shook his head, then told
Danny to stand at the
back of the hall.

'I have a very serious
announcement to make,'
began the head teacher.
'There has been an
outbreak of Penleydale
Pooping Parasite at St
Joseph's Primary School in
Burly Bottoms.'

The children tittered.

'It is not funny!' said Mr Rogers. 'And I do not
want any uncontrollable pooping in *my* school!'

At that moment Harry Hood stood up and raced
from the hall.

Mr Rogers carried on. 'I want to stress how
important it is . . .'

Lily Rushton jumped up and scurried through
the doors.

'. . . to wash your hands when you've been to . . .'

Sarwit Chudda gave a little cry of alarm and scampered off, holding on to his bottom.

'Oh no!' cried the head teacher. 'We've got the Poops!'

The outbreak was so bad that by morning break, the school had run out of toilet paper. Danny was made to stand outside the toilets like a human loo-paper dispenser, as more and more children were struck down by the Poops. The long swathes of paper wrapped around Danny's body unravelled fast. His record attempt was in tatters, just like his mummy suit.

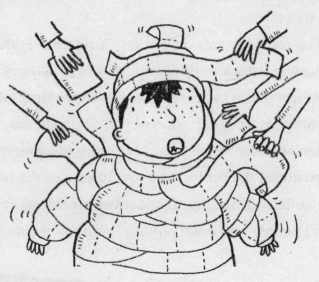

Just before home-time Matthew darted past Danny and snatched some paper from around his friend's kneecap. 'Sorry, Dan,' he said. 'It's an emergency!'

As Matthew dashed through the toilet door, 'Beaky' Rogers pinned a 'School Superstar' badge to Danny's pullover. 'You've saved the day,' he said. 'We'd have been in a bit of a pickle if you hadn't been wrapped in all that Soft and Silky!'

At that very moment, Danny felt the first gurglings and rumblings in his own tummy. 'Sorry, sir, got to go!' Danny plucked the last two squares of paper tucked inside his left sock and sprinted for the toilet.

The next day was a Saturday, and their Friday afternoon attack of the Poops was over. Danny and Matthew made their way back down Tempest Road, pushing another cart load of pongy plastic bags to throw over the Fence. Word had spread around the town about the rubbish-removing service the boys were offering, and for the past two weeks, more and more people had been paying them to take away

their litter.

'How much money have we raised now?' asked Danny.

'Four hundred and sixty-one pounds seventy-seven pence,' replied Matthew.

'Ace!' said Danny.

'Which leaves us nine-hundred and ninety-nine thousand, five hundred and thirty-eight pounds, twenty-three pence short of our target.'

'Not Ace!' said Danny.

'We've been making *some* money from the sponsored record attempts, but we're doing much better since we started shifting rubbish,' explained Matthew. 'In the three weeks since we began "Mascots in Need", we've made an average of one hundred and fifty-three pounds ninety-two pence a week. At this rate, it'll take six thousand four hundred and ninety-six weeks and four days to make a million pounds. Allowing for leap years, I've worked out it'll be Christmas 2135 before we've made enough money to save the Mascots – and we've only got a week!'

'I'll have to do more records,' said Danny. 'And fast!'

Just then he noticed a neat little man standing on a stepladder, peering over the Fence. He was wearing a yellow hard hat on his head, and a glowing orange safety jacket over his smart grey suit.

'Watch out, mister!' called Danny. 'There's a black hole down there!'

The man scrambled down the ladder and stormed up the street towards them, his teeth bared like a guard dog.

'So *you're* the ones who've been dumping refuse here without permission,' he snarled, stabbing his finger at the boys.

'We've been doing it to raise money for the Mascots in Need appeal,' explained Danny.

'*And* helping to keep Penleydale clean while the binmen are on strike,' added Matthew.

'Well, I'm Ethelred Snipe, Head of P.H.E.W.,' said the man. 'That's the Penleydale Housing, Environment and Waste department to you. I've just been informed that the strike is over. Any payment you have received from unauthorized collection of refuse rightly belongs to us and will be confiscated.'

'But we worked hard to raise that money,' said Danny. 'You can't take it from us. It belongs to the Mascots!'

'It belongs to the council,' replied Ethelred Snipe. 'Hand it over at once!'

Matthew rummaged in his pocket and pulled out four pound coins. 'This is all we've collected today,' he said.

'I'll have that!' spat Snipe, snatching the money from Matthew. 'You have a week to hand over the rest, or there will be *very* serious consequences!'

The Leaning Tower of Pizzas

Dear Mr Bibby

My record attempts keep getting scuppered.

I tried to break the Longest Time Dressed as a
Toilet-paper Mummy record, but
an outbreak of the Penleydale
Pooping Parasite at school
ruined it on day one.

loo roll

Then my Highest Leaning Tower of Pizzas
attempt was a disaster too!

Pizza Perfetto, who sponsor Penleydale United's
mascot Margarita Pizza, gave me £50, and the
owner Pasquale agreed to bake the pizzas. While
I stacked them, Matt kept a check on the

pizza-number to tower-angle ratio (whatever that means!).

I'd got the stack up to 6.45 metres when it was pounced on by a massive flock of hungry birds. In about two minutes they'd pecked our pizzas to pieces and Pasquale didn't have enough dough to start again.

Was our pizza tower the highest ever?

Best wishes
Danny Baker

PS We looked the
birds up in my
Encyclopedia of (Not
Quite) All Knowledge
and found out they

Italian
Tufty-tailed
Pizza-pecker

were Italian Tufty-tailed Pizza-peckers.

PPS The Home for Abandoned Football Mascots
is in big trouble. The council wants to pinch the
money we've earned from collecting rubbish,
but we're not giving it up without a fight. We're
starting a protest! We've even made banners —
Ace!

ARE YOU A RECORD
BREAKER ?

Dear Danny

Bad luck with your Longest Time Dressed as
a Toilet-paper Mummy record attempt. As a
matter of interest, the actual record ended in a
similar way to yours.

Tonto Snoddy of Bottom, Pennsylvania, stayed
wrapped in toilet paper for 258 days, 10 hours
and 39 minutes. His record could have lasted
even longer, but his mummy marathon was
ended by the terrible Pennsylvanian Pooping
Pandemonium of 1922, which brought the city's
drains to a standstill. Poor Tonto barricaded
himself in his house for two weeks so people
wouldn't steal his precious paper. But, when he
got the Poops, he was forced to unwrap himself
in record time – just in time!

Unfortunately, as I'm sure you already suspect, your pizza tower was nowhere near high enough to beat the current record. In May 1988, Italian chef Asti Spumanti created a record-breaking 29.45m Leaning Tower of Pizzas. Asti built his pile of pizzas next to the actual Leaning Tower of Pisa, following the 5.5 degree angle of the original exactly. He used special triple-strength mozzarella and extra oily olive oil to make the pizzas stickier, and so bind them together. An army of volunteers stood guard by Asti's tower, brandishing long breadsticks to keep pigeons, tourists, and tufty-tailed pizza-peckers away.

However, nothing could keep Paolo 'Quattro' Stagione, the Neapolitan champion pizza eater at bay. He couldn't resist the tasty feast and broke through the ring of guards, charging greedily into the teetering pizza column. The whole lot toppled over, burying Paolo completely. Miraculously he survived, and munched his way to freedom, setting a new world

record for a Pizza-pile Emergency-exit Munching
Manoeuvre.

Best wishes
Eric Bibby
Keeper of the Records

The protest banner was
ready, and everyone had
helped. Mum found an
old bed sheet and cut it
down to size. Dad nailed
the long strip of cloth
to two pieces of wood.

Danny and Matthew
painted the letters, and Natalie dabbed glittery
silver nail varnish 'to make it sparkle in the sun'.
Even baby Joey helped by dribbling on one corner.

The boys marched through town and along
Tempest Road, proudly holding the banner high in
the air. The bright red letters demanded, 'Hands Off
Our £££s!
Don't Rob the
Mascots!"

They took
up position
in front of
the Fence as,
behind them,

workmen began to dismantle it. A crowd of people soon gathered to watch the protest. Ethelred Snipe, the little man from P.H.E.W., strode towards Danny and Matthew, clutching at a clipboard as though it was a shield.

'Right, young litterbugs, your time is up,' he sneered. 'Hand over the money.'

There were cries of, 'Shame!' and, 'Boo!' from the onlookers.

'It's daylight robbery!' shouted Elsie Stubbins.

'They worked hard to raise that money!' called Vera Buggie, from the Eat Your Greens grocery shop.

The workmen moved the last four sections of the Fence, and everyone in the crowd gasped.

'Is it a tunnel to the centre of the earth?' asked Danny, craning his neck to see.

'Is it a black hole in space?' asked Matthew.

Ethelred Snipe sneered. 'Of course not!' he said. 'It's the basement of the new Toot Modern Art Gallery.'

The boys stared down into a massive cavernous

hollow in the ground. A great pyramid of pongy plastic bags rose up from the deep dark depths.

'It's a trashberg!' said Danny.

'It's a scrapheap,' corrected Mr Snipe.

'And we made it!' said Matthew proudly.

Laughter burst from the crowd, followed by loud applause.

'Bravo!' shouted Elsie Stubbins.

Mr Snipe opened his mouth to say something else, but then turned and gaped in astonishment. Danny and Matthew followed his gaze as a sound like a flock of angry geese honked at them from the top of Tempest Road.

'It's the March of the Mascots!' cried Danny.

The crowd cheered and clapped as the Great

Goalton Vuvuzela Band led Wally the Wall, Nat the Nit and a score of others towards them blowing their blaring bugles. The mascots formed a circle around the edge of the hole, surrounding the massive mound of rubbish bags and waving placards proclaiming, 'Mascots Need Mascots in Need!'

'What's going on?' spluttered Ethelred Snipe.

Moo-Moo La Moor waved a defiant hoof at him. 'If you take the money these lads have raised, you might as well chuck us on that scrapheap too!'

Willy Welly chased Mr Snipe away, with a swift kick to his bottom.

'This is most irregular!' complained the man from P.H.E.W. 'You haven't heard the last of this!'

For the rest of the week the protest continued as the mascots camped out in front of the scrapheap. The Bustagut Burger Bar supplied them with tea and burgers, while Elsie Stubbins and Vera Buggie brought them buns and bananas. Passers-by threw loose change into the Mascots in Need collection buckets.

'This is cool,' said Matthew, counting the money. 'We've already made an extra ninety-eight pounds and sixty-three pence!'

'Ace!' said Danny. 'But we're still *miles* from a million, and we've run out of time.'

After school each day the boys joined the mascots in the protest. Strangely, Mr Snipe had stayed away.

'He's up to something,' said Billy Bladder.

To keep everyone entertained, Danny practised flicking teabags into Matthew's teapot hat.

Occasionally Mum and Dad came too, pushing Baby Joey along in his pushchair. They asked Natalie to come, but

she declared that she would rather wear one of Joey's nappies on her head than be seen in public 'standing between a big toe and a giant pimple'.

The sun shone and the rubbish cooked. At first wisps of stinky purple steam began to drift upwards from the pile, like strange toxic ghosts. Danny, Matthew and the Mascots wrapped football scarves around their faces to keep the smell away. Police set up an exclusion zone of twenty-five metres around the pile, to keep spectators at a safe distance.

After days of simmering, the wisps became a solid column of dense violet fog that climbed into the sky above the town, spreading out like an umbrella over the valley. Radio Penleydale announced that planes had been ordered not to fly over the area because of the risk that the thick billowing cloud might cause an accident.

Everyone agreed that *something* had to be done. And fast.

What a Load of Rubbish!

Then one evening, something *was* done.

Ethelred Snipe stormed down the road towards the protestors, clipboard clutched firmly to his chest. Hurrying along behind him, trying to keep up, was a tall thin woman dressed in a sharp black suit and very high heels. They pushed through the crowd of people that had gathered to support the protest, and marched up to the boys.

'The P.H.E.W. committee held an emergency meeting today,' said Mr Snipe. 'We have agreed that the money you collected does indeed belong to the Mascots in Need appeal.'

A great cheer went up from the crowd. The mascots hugged each other and danced a victory jig.

'However,' continued Mr Snipe, 'so does all this rubbish.' A thin triumphant smirk spread across his face. He held out his hand to indicate the tall thin woman standing next to him. 'Let me introduce Camilla Rockyfiddler, President of the Toot Modern Art Gallery.'

The woman looked down her nose at the boys. 'This vile, stinking pile of rubbish has been thrown on to our land without my permission,' said the woman. 'I insist you remove it immediately.'

'How?' asked Danny.

'Where to?' asked Matthew.

'P.H.E.W. would be happy to take it away for you,' replied Mr Snipe. 'At a price.'

He quickly scribbled a few calculations on a piece of paper attached to his clipboard, then handed it to Danny.

PENLEYDALE HOUSING, ENVIRONMENT AND WASTE DEPARTMENT

The Town Hall, Penleydale

<u>*Estimate for Waste Removal Work:*</u>

Scoopage of waste: £8,218.03

Carriage of waste: £9,111.11

Dumpage of waste: £6,130.08

Total cost for Removage of waste:

£23,459.22 (approximately)

Ethelred Snipe

'But that's over forty times more than we've raised!' cried Matthew.

'What about the Mascots in Need appeal?' asked Danny.

Ethelred Snipe shrugged. 'That's your problem, not mine,' he said.

'Looks like we're for the scrapheap after all,' wailed Wally the Wall.

Just then a long sleek silver limo purred down Tempest Road and jolted to a sudden halt. A chauffeur got out of the car, hurried round to the rear door and opened it. A man as sleek and shiny as the limo stepped out. He wore an expensive suit and sunglasses, and his long black hair was slicked back in a ponytail.

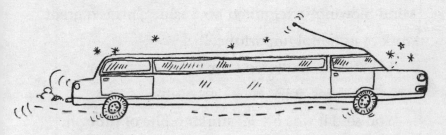

Camilla Rockyfiddler gasped. 'It's Charles Sushi, owner of the Sushi Gallery of Super-duper Art in London!' she said. 'He's the Most Important Art Expert in the World Ever.'

Charles Sushi sauntered over, pinched his nose and stared at the steaming, smelly trashberg. 'I'd heard rumours of an astounding new artwork,' he

announced, pacing up and down. 'And here it is: "The Scrapheap". What genius created this wonder?'

'We did,' said Danny and Matthew.

'Marvellous! Miraculous! Mind-blowing!' exclaimed Mr Sushi. 'This is a great work of national importance!'

'Er . . . is it?' stuttered Camilla Rockyfiddler. 'Er . . . Yes! Yes, it is!'

'You said it was a vile, stinking pile of rubbish,' said Danny.

Ms Rockyfiddler laughed nervously. 'What I meant was . . . It's a vile, stinking pile of *artistic* rubbish!'

Charles Sushi turned to Danny and Matthew. 'I want this work in *my* gallery in London,' he said. 'I will give you a hundred thousand pounds for it!'

Danny and Matthew's jaws dropped. '*How much?*'

Camilla Rockyfiddler turned to Ethelred Snipe. 'The Toot Modern *must* have it!' she hissed. 'Don't forget, Penleydale Council gave me one million pounds to spend.'

'Yes, but . . .' he began to reply, his smile suddenly gone.

'I'll give you two hundred thousand pounds!' she said to Danny and Matthew.

'*Three* hundred thousand!' bid Charles Sushi, glaring at her.

'Four hundred thousand!'

'Five hundred thousand!'

'Six hundred thousand!'

Ethelred Snipe's jaw dropped.

'*How much?*'

'Seven hundred thousand!' spat Charles Sushi.

'Eight hundred thousand!' snarled Camilla Rockyfiddler.

The Most Important Art Expert in the World Ever hesitated, his eyes blazing. 'Nine hundred thousand pounds!' he growled through clenched teeth. 'And that's my final offer.'

The President of the Toot Modern Gallery smiled triumphantly. 'One . . . million . . . pounds!'

Danny, Matthew and Ethelred's jaws dropped even further. *'How much?'*

Charles Sushi glowered at them all, speechless with rage, then stormed back into his limo and slammed the door. With a screech of wheels the car sped off down Tempest Road.

Camilla Rockyfiddler turned to Danny and Matthew. 'One million pounds,' she offered. 'Is it a deal?'

'Ask the mascots,' said Danny. 'It's *their* money.'

'Deal!' roared the mascots.

'Ace!' said Danny.

'Cool!' agreed Matthew.

'The Scrapheap will be the centrepiece of the new extension,' said Camilla Rockyfiddler, gazing in wonder at the vile, stinking pile of artistic rubbish and getting out her cheque book. 'Who do I give the money to?'

'Mascots in Need,' answered Matthew.

'They're not in need any more!' laughed Danny. 'They're saved!'

Danny Baker
Record Breaker

Dear Mr Bibby

Me and Matt have saved the Great Goalton
Home for Abandoned Football Mascots! They
got the million pounds they needed to stay open,
when the Toot Modern Art
Gallery bought our smelly
scrapheap! We've got no
idea why they wanted it,
but who cares? The mascots
are happy — they've not lost
their home, and they've still got a job! Ace!

To celebrate our victory we went for the world
record for Long-distance Spoon-launched
Used-teabag Propulsion (teapot-hat target).
Matt stood at the top of Tempest Road wearing

his teapot on his head, and I stood at the other end, outside the Crumbly Crunch biscuit factory. There were hundreds of people and mascots watching and cheering us on, so I was a bit nervous. It took me five goes, but all our practice finally paid off and I managed to ping

teabags

38.55m

a teabag 38.55 metres into the pot! Is this a record?

Best wishes
Danny Baker

The Great Big Book
of World Records
London

ARE YOU A RECORD
BREAKER ?

Dear Danny

Congratulations on raising the magnificent sum
of a million pounds: I knew you could do it!

38.55 metres was a brilliant attempt on the
Long-distance Spoon-launched Used-teabag
Propulsion (teapot-hat target) world record, but
you did not break it. The current holders are
Chinese twins Yo-Yo and Ming-Ming, of Beijing,
who broke the record quite accidentally.

In September 1997 they set out to walk along
the entire 6,259.6 km length of the Great Wall
of China, carrying their supplies on their backs
and their ceremonial teapots on their heads.
Yo-Yo was a faster walker than Ming-Ming, and
frequently strode on ahead. One morning, in

68

an attempt to get Yo-Yo's attention, Ming-Ming launched a 'Dragon in the Soup' teabag high into the air. It dropped into Yo-Yo's teapot without even touching the sides, in a record-breaking flick that measured 103.61 metres.

Don't be too disappointed, Danny, because I do have a surprise for you and Matthew. Your pile of rubbish is officially the Smelliest Artwork Ever Created: it's a record breaker! Viewers of the previous record holder – Stacy Flemmin's 'My Unflushed Toilet' – merely had to hold their noses to look at it. Her work was stinky, but not so stinky that it affected the flight paths of aircraft as your scrapheap did. Yours is a genuine masterpiece of smelly record breaking.

Please find enclosed your certificates. Well done to you both.

Best wishes
Eric Bibby
Keeper of the Records

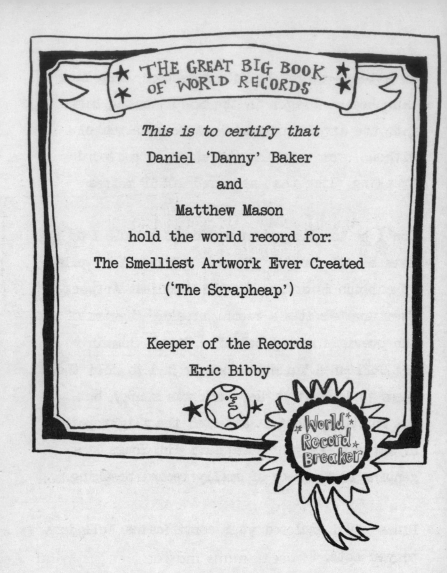

THE GREAT BIG BOOK
OF WORLD RECORDS

This is to certify that
Daniel 'Danny' Baker
and
Matthew Mason
hold the world record for:
The Smelliest Artwork Ever Created
('The Scrapheap')

Keeper of the Records
Eric Bibby

World
Record
Breaker

On their return visit to Goalton, Dad drove down the newly mended road and through the freshly painted gates. There was a shiny new sign over the entrance:

Great Goalton
Home for
Rescued Football Mascots

Natalie sulked in the back seat. 'Mum, can't we go shopping instead?'

'No,' replied Mum. 'The mascots have invited us all here to say thank you to Danny and Matthew.'

The boys were greeted like heroes. Great Goalton had been renamed, modernized and upgraded, and had gone from strength to strength. It was now home to twice as many mascots as before, and visitor numbers were up 3,689 per cent. Wally the Wall took Danny, Matthew and their families on a tour of the new facilities. Everything was bright,

new and freshly painted. There was even a new
International section, including:

Marco Il Magnifico
(a round white ball of
mozzarella cheese) from
Atletico Tonino in Italy,

Barfa (an oval-shaped
travel-sickness pill) from
Barfalona in
Spain,

Bruno o Bunda (a suntanned
bottom) from Bumfica
in Portugal,
and from
Germany
Frankie der
Frankfurter (a three-
metre-tall hot dog) from the
Frankfurt Frankfurters, and
Hammie der Hamburger, (a cheeseburger with a
gherkin) from their deadly rivals the Hamburg
Hamburgers.

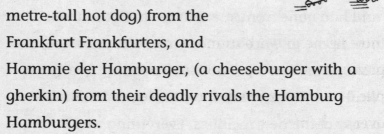

'Look out, Matt!' said Danny as a big pink prawn raced towards them. 'It's Gogo La Gamba, from Real Marisco!'

The Spanish prawn stopped in his tracks and pointed a pink rubber claw at Matthew. The last time the two had met, Matthew had accidentally pulled Gogo's tail off.

'You!' gasped Gogo.

'Me!' replied Matthew.

'Mi cola!' yelled the prawn, and scampered away holding on to his tail.

Just then, Danny saw a mound of bin liners, tatty plastic bags, banana skins, newspapers and pizza slices piled up by the exit door. Suddenly the pile of rubbish moved, sprouted legs and shuffled over to them.

'Hello, everybody,' it said. 'I'm Scrappy the Heap.'

'What are *you* doing here?' asked Natalie. 'You're the mascot for the Toot Modern Art Gallery.'

'Not any more,' said Scrappy. 'Camilla Rockyfiddler gave me the sack. Now I'm the official mascot for Mascots in Need.'

'Why did you lose your old job?' asked Mum.

'Danny and Matthew's scrapheap was so stinky that no one wanted to visit the gallery. Mr Snipe ordered the binmen to clear it out of the place and dump it on the tip.'

Danny grinned. 'So our work of art *was* just a vile, stinking pile of rubbish after all.'

Scrappy nodded. 'Unless the gallery can raise a million pounds it'll have to close down.'

'Maybe you should offer to raise money for *them*,' said Dad.

'Yeah,' laughed Danny. 'Let's call it "Toot Aid"!'

As they were about to leave for home, Wally the Wall presented the boys with free admission for life, gave them goody-bags full of souvenirs, and autographed postcards of all the mascots. Danny chuckled as he had a special one signed for Natalie.

'Mum!' she whined. 'Tell him!'

The
Rip-Roaring
Raspberry

WARNING!
High Winds
Ahead!

Bogey Flicking

THE PENLEYDALE CLARION

QUEEN TO VISIT PENLEYDALE!

It was announced yesterday that Her Majesty the Queen will visit Penleydale Town Centre in two weeks' time to open Crumbly Crunch's new dog-biscuit factory. She will be bringing her favourite corgi Nanki-Poo

HRH NANKI-POO

on the visit. The dog has reportedly swallowed the Queen's favourite jewel, the Pimple of the Raj, said to be worth £75,466,342.51. This famous pink diamond was given to the Queen by the Maharaja of Eysore, to celebrate her Golden Jubilee.

PIMPLE oF THE RAJ

'The jewel has become lodged in the animal's lower intestine,' said Royal Veterinary Professor Donald Merryweather. 'We are waiting for nature to take its course.'

Fred Flatfoot, Managing Director of Crumbly Crunch, said, 'If the royal pooch hasn't produced a little parcel by the time Her Majesty arrives, we would be honoured to present her with a commemorative box of our new Runnybum medicinal dog biscuits – 'guaranteed to keep doggy bottoms happy!'

THE DIAMOND INSIDE
NANKI-POO'S GUT

Mayor Alfred Trott promised that the royal visitors would get a typical Penleydale welcome. 'There are plans for tea-slurping and biscuit-dunking demonstrations,' he said. 'And a re-enactment of the 1698 Pigling's Pit witch trials.'

After the ceremony to open the new factory, the Miggins' Mop Cloggers will dance for the Queen before she carries on to Saltimuchty in Scotland to see the annual Ben Doone Highland Kilt-swishing Jamboree.

Bogey Flicking

To The Keeper of the Records
The Great Big Book of World Records
London

Dear Mr Bibby

I'm in a bit of a pickle. I've
been wearing my new 'Stick-
like-glue' goalkeeping gloves
twenty-four hours a day to

nose
picking

make them fit like a second skin (well, that's
what it says on the box!). I've not let in a goal
since I started wearing them. I'm on a roll, so
I don't want to take the gloves off.

The trouble is, I'm practising for the County
Bogey-flicking Championships and they're
affecting my form. I can get distance, but
I can't get accuracy. I was entered for the

junior ten-metre target-flicking event, but now I'm thinking of going for the long-distance award instead.

Yesterday I sent one of my practice bogeys a distance of 39.77 metres! I'm sure a tournament-grade bogey will go further, but I don't want to use the ones I've been rolling and polishing for the championships, in case I spoil them.

Bogeys

stick-like-glue

39.77 m!

Have I broken a record already?

Best wishes
Danny Baker

ARE YOU A RECORD
BREAKER ?

Dear Danny

It's great to see you've revived your interest
in nose-picking! Surprisingly the Grand
National Bogey-flicking Society regulations
allow flickers to compete either with or
without gloves. The trick is to find material
that gives just the right amount of bogey
adhesion (stickiness) without sacrificing
accuracy or distance. Traditional flickers say
that the human fingernail does this anyway and
so compete au naturel.

Obviously your 'Stick-like-glue' gloves are not
good for accurate flicking but have produced
a fantastic long-distance attempt. However, you
are still short of the world record of 63.28
metres, held by the Grand Master Flickerman

Henri Le Hooter, of Le Pic, in France.

Henri was born to be a bogey-flicking champion.
He had an immense cavernous nose that
naturally produced top-grade bogeys, and an
unnaturally long springy middle finger on his
right hand that launched his mini-missiles with
terrific speed, precision and distance. As well as
holding the long-distance record he is the only
man ever to achieve a perfect score at five, ten
and twenty-metre target flicking.

Perhaps your tournament-grade bogeys will give
you the extra distance you need. Good luck!

Best wishes
Eric Bibby
Keeper of the Records

PS I thought you'd like
to see a photo of Henri
caught in mid-flick.

Danny balanced a practice bogey on the end of his second finger, took aim at the target and flicked. The little green ball sailed down the hallway and stuck high up on the wall, joining a scattering of others which were splattered everywhere except on the target.

Matthew's bogeys were all grouped nicely in or around the bullseye.

'It's no good, Dan,' said Matthew. 'You're not going to win the target championships with your "Stick-like-glue" goalkeeping gloves on.' Danny flicked again. The small green blob skewed way to the left. It reached the kitchen door at exactly the same moment Danny's sister walked through it, and landed on her chin. Natalie was listening to her favourite band, *Boy$!!!,* and didn't notice the bogey. She strolled past Danny and Matthew singing tunelessly, opened the front door and went out.

'Where's Nat the Brat going?' asked Matthew.

'She's got a new boyfriend – *Sebastian,*' replied Danny, making a face. 'They're going to the cinema to see *Kisses for My Sweetheart.*'

'Mega-gross!' said Matthew, pretending to be sick.

'Ziga-giga-piga-gross!' corrected Danny. 'I bet *he'd* rather see *The End of the World Part 7.*'

'What happened to her last boyfriend?' asked Matthew.

'He dumped her after I gave them both nits.'

Matthew laughed. 'What's this one going to say when she turns up with a big bogey on her face?'

Danny grinned and was about to answer, when Mum came into the hall carrying baby Joey in one arm. The wrist she had sprained mending the washing machine was heavily bandaged.

'If you've got nothing better to do than flick

bogeys,' she said,
'you can take Joey to
playgroup at Matthew's
house. Matt's mum has
offered to look after
him for a few hours
each day, because I'm
struggling to do things
at the moment with my wrist being like this.'

'OK,' said Danny, taking the baby from Mum
and placing him in his buggy.

Danny tickled his brother's tummy playfully.
Joey chuckled and then let loose a ferocious
rumbling trump that rocketed his pushchair
backwards.

'Ace!' said Danny.

'Cool,' agreed Matthew.
'Does he
always do
that when
you tickle his
tummy?'

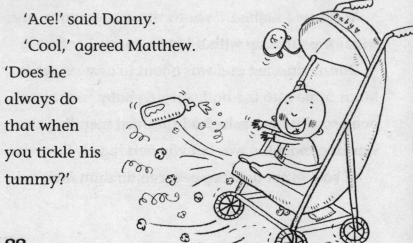

'He does when he's just had Barleybricks and milk,' laughed Mum. 'Tracy Wilkins said her baby Tom does it when he's had strawberry yogurt.'

Joey kicked his feet happily and gurgled.

'You were just the same, Danny,' continued Mum. 'When you were nine months old, you trumped so hard you blew a hole in your nappy.'

'Ace! Do you think it was the Biggest Baby-bottom-burp Ever?'

'I don't know,' laughed Mum. 'It was definitely a ripper!'

'Hey, Matt,' said Danny as the boys pushed Joey over to Matthew's house. 'How many babies do your mum and her friend look after?'

'About six or seven. Why?'

'Let's find out what makes each one trump, and have a poot-powered pushchair race!'

The boys spent the afternoon checking what each baby had to eat or drink and if it made them windy. Matthew drew up a chart so that he could pinpoint which foods produced the biggest trumps and how to trigger them. He even interviewed the

mums when they came to collect their children at the end of the day, scribbling down the answers on his sheet.

'Now I know what each baby needs,' said Matthew, 'I've asked the mums to give each one their own special fart-food tomorrow.'

'Ace!' said Danny. 'Then we can have the race.'

When he got home and pushed Baby Joey into the hallway, Natalie was staring at herself in the mirror with a look of horror on her face.

'How long has *this* been on my chin?' she screeched, pointing to the bogey.

Danny shrugged. 'A while.'

'I wondered why Sebastian kept staring at me,'

wailed Natalie. 'I thought it was because I looked beautiful, but all the time he was just staring at your horrible disgusting bogey!'

She lunged for Danny's ears in a desperate attempt to pull them off, but he used Joey's buggy as a shield, manoeuvring it between him and his angry sister. They chased each other around the hallway, Natalie hopping and grabbing, Danny ducking and weaving, baby Joey gurgling and giggling.

Danny managed to get to the bottom of the stairs, and fled to the safety of his room.

'You're cat meat, Danny Baker!' screamed his sister.

Baby Bottom Burps

Dear Mr Bibby

I think my baby brother
Joey's going to be a
record breaker, just like
me.

This morning, me and Matt organized a fart-
propelled pushchair competition between all the
babies at the playgroup. We found out what
made each baby really
trumpy and made sure
they all had that for
lunch. Then we lined them
all up in their pushchairs
on the patio in Matthew's
back garden and pulled

3·76m!

their trump-triggers.

Joey needs his tummy tickled,
Ryan Drabble needs his toes
tapped, Tom Wilkins needs
his nose nudged, Harry
Bickerstaff needs his knees
knocked and Willy Green just
went off by himself!

We couldn't make the girl babies trump - it
must be a boy thing.

Joey won the competition bottoms down! He
managed to make his pushchair roll 7.88 metres,
beating Harry Bickerstaff by a massive 3.76
metres. I'm so proud of him. Has he broken a
record?

Best wishes
Danny Baker

PS I've decided to stick with my Stick-like-glue gloves and just go for the long-distance event at the County Bogey-flicking Championships. They're too Ace to take off!

PPS My football team, the Coalclough Sparrows, only needs to win two more games to do the league and cup double again.

PPPS I think Walchester United scouts are watching me play. Dad's the club's goalkeeping coach, but he says I'm still not old enough to be in the youth squad. I think he's kidding me so that I don't get nervous. Fingers crossed!

The Great Big Book
of World Records
London

ARE YOU A RECORD
BREAKER ?

Dear Danny

Baby Joey's windy bottom shows fantastic
promise, but his Single-emission Flatulence-
propelled Pushchair Locomotion distance of 7.88
metres was not quite enough to beat the world
record.

The current record was set by a ten-month-old
baby, Berti Blunderbuss, of Mönchengladbach,
Germany. His father, Wilhelm, invented a special
exhaust system on Berti's pushchair that
concentrated the wind into a fast-flowing jet
stream. This acted like a rocket thruster and,
when combined with a special baby diet of
cauliflower and cabbage curry, drove little
Berti a whopping distance of 23.13 metres.

Wilhelm then adapted Berti's pushchair so that it could be steered by remote control. On 2 June 2004 he guided the baby around the Olympic Stadium in Munich to a Repeated Multiple-emission Flatulence-propelled Pushchair Locomotion world record of 603.52 metres, which only ended when Baby Berti ran out of gas.

Perhaps Matthew could construct a similar exhaust system for Joey's pushchair and Joey could have another attempt?

Best wishes
Eric Bibby
Keeper of the Records

PS Good luck in your last two games, Danny. I wouldn't be surprised if Walchester United are watching you play. You deserve to get selected.

Natalie strolled into the kitchen and tweaked Danny's left ear.

'Ow!' he cried. 'Stop doing that!'

'After what you did when I went out with Sebastian, I'm *never* going to stop,' she replied. 'I'm going to carry on until you've got two great big cauliflower ears!'

Mum smiled. 'Just make one of them into a cauliflower, Natalie,' she said. 'Turn the other into a carrot.'

Natalie pulled her tongue out at Danny and grabbed a piece of his breakfast toast. 'They just said on the news that the Queen's corgi has still not done its business,' she announced.

Dad rolled his eyes as he picked up his car keys to leave for work. 'Nat, do you *have* to give us a daily update on the constipated corgi?'

'The Nation's holding its breath,' she replied. 'Aren't you?'

'No!' they all chorused.

Matthew arrived after breakfast. Danny picked up Joey and the three boys escaped into the living

room until Dad and Natalie had gone out and
Mum was having a bath.

'Hey, Matt,' said Danny, strapping his baby
brother into his pushchair. 'Look at this.'

Danny squatted down in front of Joey and gently
pushed his little button nose. Joey frowned for a
moment, then suddenly let fly with a big booming
burp. The force of it blew Danny's hair back from
his face and made the living-room curtains ripple,
like a kite catching the wind.

Mum's best
flower vase rocked
on the windowsill.
It teetered . . . and
tottered . . . then
toppled towards
the floor.

Danny dived across the room, as
though he was stretching along his goal line to save
a shot. Luckily he was still wearing his Stick-like-
glue goalkeeping gloves and grabbed the vase just
before it smashed on to the carpet.

'Great save, Dan!'
cried Matthew.

'I told you,' replied
Danny, clutching the
vase to his chest. 'These
are my lucky gloves.
Nothing can get past me
while I'm wearing them.'

He replaced the ornament on the
windowsill, then gazed at his brother.

'That was a corker!' he said. 'It was his loudest
yet! He burps like that after he's eaten a jar of
sloppy mango and kiwi fruit baby dinner.'

'He's awesome!' said Matthew.

'Come on,' said Danny. 'Let's
take him to playgroup. That's
not all he can do. I'll show you
more on the way – it's safer
outdoors!'

As the boys turned the corner
at the end of Danny's street they spotted a small
crowd of people staring and pointing up into a tree.

'What's the matter?' asked Danny, when they reached the group.

'My Tiddles has got herself stuck up the tree,' sobbed old Mrs Wigglesworth.

Danny looked into the thick ball of green leaves, and could just see a small black and white kitten clinging to one of the highest branches. It mewed pitifully.

'We need a ladder,' said a man in the crowd.

'No, we should call the fire brigade,' said a woman.

'Poke the poor thing with a long stick, and catch her in a blanket,' suggested a girl.

I wonder . . . thought Danny. He tipped Baby Joey's pushchair back so that his brother was looking up into the tree.

'Matt, keep the buggy tilted like this,' he said.

When Matt had got a firm hold of the handles,

Danny gave
Joey's tummy
a quick tickle.
Joey
gurgled
happily,
then BOOM!
Another
ferocious belch
exploded from his mouth.

The branches of the tree swayed and jumped.
The leaves quivered and hissed. Poor Tiddles
miaowed loudly, trying to cling on to the bending,
bouncing branch, but she lost her grip and tumbled
from the tree.

Danny moved quickly, leaping with his hands
outstretched. The kitten dropped towards the
ground and smack   straight into the safety of
Danny's Stick-like-glue gloves.

'You're my hero!' cried Mrs Wigglesworth, taking
Tiddles from Danny. She stared at Joey. 'And that
baby's dynamite!'

'What else can he do?' asked Matthew as they went on their way.

'Watch,' replied Danny, glancing up and down the street to check if it was safe.

He reached into the pocket on the back of the buggy, pulled out a baby bottle full of peach juice and let Joey guzzle about half of it. The baby's mouth was wet and sloppy with a mixture of drool and dribbled juice.

 Just then a boy swaggered and strutted towards them. It was Maradona Potts, the school bully, who wanted Danny's place as goalkeeper in the Coalclough Sparrows team.

'Oi! Baker! Mason!' yelled Potts, grinning stupidly at them. 'Are you playing Mumsies and Dadsies with the little baby?'

'No,' replied Danny. 'We were taking him to the zoo to look at the monkeys, but we needn't bother now you're here.'

Potts glanced at Danny's goalkeeping gloves. 'Huh, I see you're wearing your cheating gloves,' he sneered. 'You're rubbish without those.'

Danny reached down and gave Joey's big toe a sharp tug.

His baby brother frowned for a moment.

His lips began to quiver.

Little bubbles grew and popped in the sloppy drool around his mouth. Then Joey took a deep breath and blew a ripping, roaring raspberry.

The loud vibrating whine seemed to make the air ripple. From close range it was devastating. Potts was knocked backwards by the force of the blast while being splattered by a shower of thick, sticky baby-drool.

The droplets enveloped him from head to toe, and in seconds Potts became a wet, shiny mess of dripping peach-flavoured spit.

'Gross!' wailed Potts.

'Ace!' laughed Danny.

'Cool,' agreed Matthew.

'You'll be sorry about this, Baker,' threatened Potts before staggering stickily away.

'How did you get Joey to do that?' asked Matthew.

'I just give him something to drink, pull his big toe and bingo!' replied Danny. 'He's getting better at it every time. Could you make a gadget to measure raspberries? Joey's might be world-beaters!'

'You mean a sort of . . . ripple-gauge?'

'Yeah!' said Danny. 'A *raspberry ripple-gauge!*'

Rippers!

Dear Mr Bibby

My baby brother Joey's
trouser-tearing trumps,
belly-busting belches and
rip-roaring raspberries are
Mega Ace! His burps can
knock cats out of trees
and clean dirty buildings!

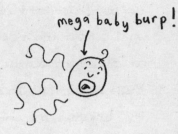

mega baby burp!

rescued cat

Ace Trumps

The town
centre's
full of workmen trying to make
Penleydale look pretty for the
Queen's visit. Yesterday, the high-
power jet-washer cleaning the
old part of the Crumbly Crunch biscuit factory
broke down.

I pointed Joey at the building and pushed his nose. The burp he did was so powerful it blasted a big patch of dirt off the wall. I kept aiming Joey at different parts of

Queen

Nanki-Poo

the mucky wall and pressing his nose. In no time the bricks were shining like new!

Surely these MUST be the Most Powerful Baby Burps Ever.

Best wishes
Danny Baker

PS I'm working on Joey's raspberry-blowing technique. When they're as powerful as I can get them, I'll let you know.

PPS I'm sure the Walchester United scouts are checking me out. A man has been standing behind my goal during our last few games and taking notes. He even did it all the way through the cup final against the Burley Bulldozers yesterday (we bulldozed them, by three goals to nil!). Dad still says United can't take me on, but I think he's just trying to keep me focused.

THE
★GREAT★
BIG
★BOOK OF★
WORLD
RECORDS

ARE YOU A RECORD
BREAKER?

Dear Danny

Joey certainly is a very talented (and windy!)
baby, and shows all the hallmarks of following
in your footsteps as a record breaker, but not
just yet. His Infant Oral Gastric Gas Expulsions
('Baby Burps') are extraordinary, but I'm afraid
they are still not record breakers.

The Yukimuki people from the Andes Mountains
in South America trained their infants to belch
in short and long bursts, like morse code, so
that they could communicate to each other
across the deep valleys. They fed the babies
on the fruit of the rare Lubiloo tree, and
this diet produced such powerful burps that
residents of villages three kilometres apart
could easily chat to each other.

In November 1927 six-month-old Tarti Tutete
burped a 'Happy Birthday' message to her
Aunty Wibi 7.65 km away. Because of the distance
involved, her father squeezed the baby's right
knee very hard. The resulting gas expulsion
was so powerful it triggered an eruption in El
Fuego, a dormant volcano situated between the
two villages.

The Tribe took this as a message from the gods
to stop their unique form of communication and
took to writing letters and sending birthday
cards instead.

Does Baby Joey have any more windy talents
hidden in his little body, I wonder?

Best wishes
Eric Bibby
Keeper of the Records

Danny and Matthew had been swimming at the Sports Centre, and strolled back along Tempest Road. An overpowering smell of fresh paint drifted over the town centre. Council workers in glowing orange jackets were out in force, painting lamp posts, fences and doors, scrubbing pavements and sweeping the roads along the route the Queen would take.

'Look!' said Matthew, pointing to a man standing beneath a tree. 'They're even painting the leaves a brighter shade of green!'

'We'd better not stand still, Matt,' said Danny, 'or they'll paint us too.'

'She'll only be here for a couple of hours,' replied his friend. 'Everyone's gone bonkers.'

'Nat has,' said Danny. 'She's obsessed with Nanki-Poo's Number Twos.'

'Is the corgi *still* bunged up?'

'Yeah, and Nat's desperate for him to poop a pile in Penleydale.'

The boys stopped to collect Baby Joey from Matthew's house. As Danny strapped his little

brother into the buggy, Matthew went up to his
bedroom. He returned a minute later carrying a
microphone that had an old lampshade around
it. A long cable went to a black box with a dial, a
timer, two switches and a
big red button on it.

'Is that it?' asked
Danny, staring
at the
contraption.

'Yeah, it's
the Raspberry
Ripple-gauge,'
replied Matthew. 'It'll
measure everything
except spitty sprays – I'm still working on that!'

'Ace!' laughed Danny. 'Come on, let's go to my
house and try it out.'

About a dozen plastic bottles were dotted around
the lawn in Danny's back garden. Four had been
knocked over.

'What's going on?' asked Matthew.

'I've been training Joey,' explained Danny. 'His raspberry-blowing's getting really accurate. If we can increase the power, he'll be deadly!'

'Then fetch some juice and let's get started.'

Danny hurried off into the kitchen while Matthew positioned Joey near Dad's shed, facing the house. He stood at the other end of the garden on the patio, holding the Raspberry Ripple-gauge. Danny returned, gave the baby a drink of peach juice, knelt down behind the buggy and tweaked his brother's big toe.

Joey gurgled happily and then let rip. The raspberry rumbled from his lips and sent a shockwave rippling across the grass towards Matthew. It scattered three of the bottles, roared over the garden gnome standing beneath the tree, shattering his pointy hat, blasted the petals from a rosebush and popped all the buttons from Matthew's shirt.

Matthew laughed, flicked a switch, pressed the red button and studied the dial. 'That had a velocity index of 2,399 and a vibration index of 1,585,' he said. 'Giving a Total Rip Index of 3,984!'

'*That,*' said Danny. 'Was a gnome-gnasher!'

At that moment Natalie stormed out of the patio door. 'What was that noise?' she said. 'I was just about to get an update on Nanki-Poo's bottom trouble when the telly conked out!'

Danny saw his chance. He gave Joey another sip of peach juice, hid behind the pushchair and pulled the toe-trigger.

A cloud of baby spit sprayed from Joey's quivering lips as the raspberry zipped and sped like a racing car towards the house. The rippling air stripped leaves from the tree and cut a swathe along the lawn, like an invisible mower speeding towards Natalie.

Danny's sister stood frozen with horror as she

was hit by the full force of the wet, viciously-vibrating raspberry. Her hair stood on end, her clothes shimmered and flapped, and with a 'ping' the elastic in her knickers snapped. Her pants fell down and lay in a pink frilly heap around her ankles.

'Urgh!' she cried, gazing with disgust at her slobber-splattered shirt. 'Mum!' she yelled, hitching up her knickers and running into the house. 'Tell him!'

'*That* had a velocity index of 4,671 and vibration index of 3,988, giving a Total Rip Index of 8,659!' said Matthew, examining the dials and timer on the Raspberry Ripple-gauge.

'*That* was a knicker-buster!' laughed Danny,

pointing at the wall of the house. 'And a sister-splatterer – look!'

The fine spray of baby-drool had left a perfect silhouette of Natalie on the brickwork.

The boys stared at Joey, who was blowing bubbles and kicking his feet merrily at the far end of the garden.

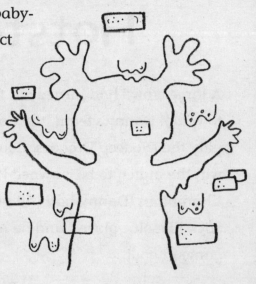

'He's awesome,' said Matthew.

'He's Ace!' corrected Danny.

The Hotspoon Hotstars

A large crowd had turned out the next morning to watch Danny's team, the Coalclough Sparrows, play the Digdeep Dingoes. Coalclough needed to win the match to be crowned Penleydale League Champions. Danny had still not taken off his lucky Stick-like-glue gloves, and he had another great game in goal.

It was a close match. Two goals by Matthew and Jimmy Sedgley late in the first half, gave the Sparrows an advantage. In the second half the Dingoes threw everything they had at Danny, but he caught every cross and saved every shot. Coalclough were the Champions once again.

The Lord Mayor of Penleydale presented the team with their medals, then handed the trophy to Matthew, the captain of the Coalclough Sparrows. The crowd cheered and clapped as he held the cup high.

Dad ruffled Danny's hair. 'Well done,' he said. 'You played a blinder.'

Later, at home, Danny was telling his mum all the details of the game when there was a knock at the door. A minute later Dad came into the room with the man Danny had seen watching him play.

'Danny, this is Bill Biggins,' said Dad. 'He wants a word with you.'

'Hello, lad,' said the man. 'You're the best young keeper I've ever seen. You haven't signed for Walchester United yet, have you?'

'Thanks, Mr Biggins. No, I haven't.' Danny's tummy tingled with excitement. This was it!

'Well, I scout for Totterton Hotspoons, looking for great new players. We'd like to make you an offer to join us on our Hotspoon Hotstars youth squad.'

Danny's jaw dropped. 'But Totterton are Walchester's deadly rivals!' he exclaimed.

Bill Biggins smiled. 'The Hotspoons want the best,' he said, slapping a contract on the table. 'And we want you. What do you say, lad?'

Danny didn't know *what* to say. He wanted to play for his dad's club, Walchester United.

'If I play for Totterton I might help them beat Walchester,' he replied. 'That *wouldn't* be Ace!'

'It would be for us!' laughed Bill Biggins, turning to Dad. 'Let me know your decision in a day or two, Mr Baker.'

When he had gone, the family sat in silence, each lost in their own thoughts.

Natalie spoke first.

'Isn't it exciting?' she said. 'The Queen's corgi

might do a number two in our town!'

'Nat!' they all chorused.

After tea, Danny and Matthew headed towards
Tempest Road to see how the preparations were
coming on for the Queen's visit. Danny filled his
friend in about the offer from Totterton Hotspoons.

'What are you going to do?' asked Matthew as
they turned the corner from the High Street.

'I don't know,' replied Danny. 'Dad says
Walchester United
haven't signed me
because the junior
team's full. I'd have to
wait until the goalie
moves up into the
senior squad.'

'They must be mad
not to sign you anyway!'
said Matthew, glancing
down at Danny's hands.

'By the way, you're not going to take those gloves

off until after the cup final, are you?'

'Don't worry, Matt. If my form carries on like it is, I might *never* take them off!'

The boys gaped as they stared down Tempest Road towards the biscuit factory.

'They've carpeted the street!' exclaimed Matthew.

The whole of Tempest Road had been covered in a bright red carpet which was being carefully vacuumed by two council workers.

Danny shrugged. 'That must be for Nanki-Poo,' he said. 'You can't have the Most Expensive Doggy-doo Ever just being dropped on to the street!'

Dog-napped!

Everything was ready for the Queen's visit, and Penleydale looked lovely. Union Jack flags fluttered in the morning breeze, and brightly coloured bunting hung in merry criss-cross lines across the streets. Even now a few orange-coated council workers scurried up and down the road doing some last-minute polishing and picking up litter.

On Tempest Road, where the Crumbly Crunch biscuit factory stood, the smell of dog biscuits filled the air. A brass band played and children frolicked on a huge inflatable Runnybum medicinal dog biscuit. Jelly-jugglers and banana-balancers kept the hundreds of people lining the roadside entertained while they waited for the Queen's car to arrive.

Danny, Matthew and their families joined the crowds on Tempest Road, standing right at the front just outside the factory gates.

'We'll get a fantastic view from here,' said

Natalie, scanning the crowd for photographers.

Mum rummaged in her bag and handed cartons
of juice to Danny, Matthew and Natalie. Danny
was still wearing his Stick-like-glue gloves, so
Matthew had to help him stick the straw into the
top of the carton. Mum bent down and gave Joey
his mid-morning bottle of milk.

'Uh-oh,' whispered Matthew. 'You said he'd had
Bran Crisps and peach juice for breakfast. If my

calculations are right, Bran Crisps, peach juice and milk are Joey's most explosive raspberry-making combo.'

'Have you got the Raspberry Ripple-gauge?' asked Danny.

'Yeah,' replied Matthew, pulling the contraption out of a plastic carrier bag. 'I thought that once we've seen the Queen, we could go to the park and see what Joey can produce this time.'

Just then Danny heard cheering coming from the top of the road and saw the Queen's limousine slow down and pull up to a stop. The chauffeur opened one of the rear doors and Her Majesty

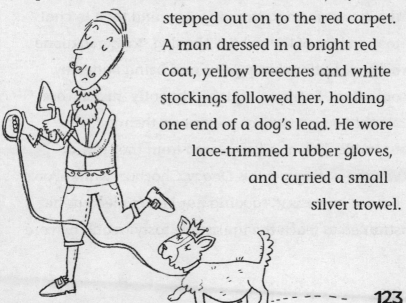

stepped out on to the red carpet. A man dressed in a bright red coat, yellow breeches and white stockings followed her, holding one end of a dog's lead. He wore lace-trimmed rubber gloves, and carried a small silver trowel.

'That's the Lord High Master of the Silver Poop Scoop,' said Natalie. 'The official Royal Pooper Scooper.'

The cheering got louder as the jewel-munching corgi waddled from the royal limousine, his tummy as big and round as a beach ball.

'I hope the corgi does its business in front of *us*,' squealed Natalie, furiously waving her flag. 'I want to see the famous diamond! I might get my picture in *Hi!* magazine.'

Danny and Matthew glanced at each other and rolled their eyes.

The Queen strolled along Tempest Road towards the biscuit factory, stopping now and then to chat to members of the public. The dog staggered along behind, sniffing lamp posts and being patted by onlookers. Everyone watched intently, just in case Nanki-Poo left a royal present on the road.

Suddenly a hand appeared from the crowd waving a Waggywoofs Doggy Chocbar. Nanki-Poo lunged towards it, tugging hard on his lead as he strained to reach the irresistible tasty treat. The Lord

High Master of the Silver Poop Scoop was caught off balance and tumbled to the ground.

At that moment another hand shot out holding a pair of scissors, and in a flash had snipped through the lead. The corgi shot towards the Chocbar, and straight into the arms of one of the council workers that had been collecting litter.

He lifted Nanki-Poo into the air and tossed the startled animal to another worker standing at the back of the crowd. The dog was passed like a rugby ball from one orange-jacketed man to another right down the street.

'They're not from the council,' gasped Matthew.

'They're robbers!' shouted Danny. 'Nanki-Poo's being dog-napped!'

The royal corgi was caught by the final member of the gang, who dived into the back seat of a waiting getaway car. The rest of the gang followed soon after and, with squealing wheels, the car sped up Tempest Road and towards the High Street.

Danny saw onlookers scatter in all directions to get out of the way. A police car drove across the top of the road, blocking the robbers' exit. The getaway car screeched in a circle, its smoking tyres leaving long curving black lines on the smooth red carpet as it roared back towards Danny – and the Queen.

Danny had to act fast. He moved Joey's pushchair into position, pointing it up and across the road. As the speeding motor car closed in on them he gave the baby's toe a sharp tug. The dangerous combination of Bran Crisps, peach juice and milk worked its

magic. Joey gurgled, then let rip with a *humongous* raspberry.

It was booming.

It was vibrating.

It was devastating.

The little triangular flags, flying high above the street, were torn from the bunting and fluttered in the air like huge multi-coloured butterflies. On the far side of the road belts snapped and trousers dropped. Hats flew and hair stood on end. Spectators were drenched in a thick mist of peach-scented baby-drool.

As the getaway car zoomed past, its tyres and windscreen exploded with the force and impact of Joey's rip-roaring raspberry. The driver lost control and the car swerved and skidded, ploughing into the massive inflatable Runnybum dog biscuit.

The constipated corgi catapulted through the hole where the windscreen had been, bounced on to the big bouncy biscuit and somersaulted serenely into the spit-saturated sky.

'Help!' cried the Queen as the flying pooch plummeted towards the ground. 'Somebody save my Nanki-Poo!'

The Corgi Has Landed

Danny shot from the crowd as though coming off his goal line to take a cross. He watched the dog's flight across the street. Judging his leap to perfection, Danny dived and plucked the corgi from the air. They tumbled on to the hard surface of the road, but Nanki-Poo stuck fast in Danny's Stick-like-glue goalkeeping gloves.

Matthew helped Danny to his feet. 'Good job I had the Raspberry Ripple-gauge switched on,' he said. 'That was Joey's best by a mile.'

Danny's knee was grazed and bleeding and his T-shirt was torn. He placed the trembling and terrified corgi gently on the ground.

Nanki-Poo whined. His eyes widened and nature took its course.

The no-longer-constipated corgi did a ripping roaring bottom-raspberry. His swollen tummy deflated like a balloon as he delivered a monstrous

Royal Whoopsie right at the boys' feet.

'Hooray!' cried Natalie, looking round and smiling in case a photographer from *Hi!* magazine was snapping the momentous event. 'Nanki-Poo's done a Number Two!'

Danny looked down at the huge steaming pile. 'That's not a Number Two,' he said. 'That's a Number Forty-two!'

'And look!' exclaimed Matthew, pointing. There
on the top, like a cherry on a cake, was the Pimple
of the Raj.

Policemen swarmed across the road to arrest
the dog-nappers and, as they were led away in
handcuffs, Danny limped back to his family.

Dad ruffled his hair. 'What a save!'

Danny grinned, and was about to reply, when he
saw the Queen walking towards them.

The Lord High Master of the Silver
Poop Scoop swooped into poop-
scooping action. In moments he
had cleared up Nanki-Poo's
majestic mess, including
the glistening, glittering
pink jewel. He stood to
attention behind the
Queen, with the corgi's
pongy parcel balanced
precariously on the end
of his shining silver
trowel.

Danny bowed awkwardly.

'Well done, young man,' said the Queen. 'What is your name?'

'Danny Baker, Your Majesty.'

'Are you hurt?'

'Not really . . . thank you,' replied Danny.

'What on earth did you use to make the fearful noise that stopped those terrible men making off with my Nanki-Poo?'

'My brother Joey,' replied Danny. 'His raspberries are like dynamite. I've been training him to produce them whenever I want.'

The Queen spoke quietly to her lady-in-waiting, who hurried over to the royal limousine, returning a few moments later with a long thin sword.

'Kneel down on one knee, young man,' ordered Her Majesty.

Danny did as he was told. 'Are you going to chop my head off?' he asked, staring anxiously at his mum and dad.

'Goodness gracious, no! This is my Emergency Knighting Sword.'

She tapped Danny gently with the blade on each shoulder. 'For gallant service to Queen and country,' she said. 'Arise, *Sir* Danny Baker.'

'Mega Ace!' cried Danny.

'Mega Cool!' agreed Matthew.

'Huh!' grumbled Natalie. 'There's no way *I'm* calling you "Sir"!'

The Queen turned to Joey. 'And as for *this* heroic baby boy,' she proclaimed, 'I award you the title

of Joey Baker, M.R.R.R.: Master of the Rip-roaring Raspberry!'

She smiled and tickled his tummy. Joey gurgled and produced a fearsome trump, driving his buggy backwards along the road. Instinctively the Queen reached out and made a grab for his feet, but only managed to tug his big toe.

Joey gurgled once more and lived up to his new title: he blew another mighty raspberry, knocking Her Majesty's vivid pink hat right off her head and enveloping her in a glistening sheen of baby-spit. The hat twirled towards Nanki-Poo's diamond-topped dollop, still perched on the end of the Lord High Master of the Silver Poop Scoop's trowel.

Again Danny launched himself into the air, reaching and stretching, and once more his Stick-like-glue goalkeeping gloves didn't let him down.

He snatched the Queen's flying hat just before it landed in Nanki-Poo's Number Two. 'Sir Danny, you *must* be the Best Goalkeeper in the World

Ever,' said Her Majesty, taking the hat from him. 'And your brother *must* be the World's Windiest Baby!'

'*I* think he is, Your Majesty,' said Danny. 'But I need to check with Mr Bibby first!'

Danny Baker
Record Breaker

Dear Mr Bibby

I had a really busy day
yesterday. I rescued the
Queen's Nanki-Poo from a
gang of evil dog-nappers,
cured his constipation,
saved the Pimple of the
Raj and got Knighted. All before lunch!

dog-napped

My brother Joey blew a
raspberry that crashed
the robber's getaway car.
Luckily Matt measured it
with his Raspberry Ripple-
gauge. It registered a
windscreen-smashing,

Raspberry
Ripple-gauge

tyre-popping, robber-stopping 14,719 on the Rip
Index!

It was a Right Royal Ripper! Has
my baby brother broken a
world record this time?

Record
Breaker?

Best wishes
Sir Danny Baker

ARE YOU A RECORD
BREAKER ?

Dear Sir Danny

I saw the news report on TV about your heroic
rescue of the Queen's corgi. Well done!

I'm delighted to tell you that baby Joey
is finally a record breaker. His rip-roaring
robber-stopper easily breaks the previous
record for Reverberating Lip-resonance
Generation (Raspberry-blowing).

The holder was Chief Ulalu Tonka of the small
Muddi tribe of Africa. The men used to insert
large wooden plates into their upper and lower
lips. When combined with a special drink made
from goat's milk and juju juice, these lip-
plates enabled them to produce lethal hunting
raspberries. Individual men could bring down

flying birds. As a group, the loud fast-flapping
lip-vibrating twang produced by the hunters
could stop a full-grown rhino in its tracks.

In 1956, Chief Ulalu Tonka generated a single
raspberry that registered a Total Rip Index
of 10,888, but which blew apart the walls of
his house, bringing the roof crashing down on
top of him and pulverizing everything inside.
When rescuers searched the rubble, all they
could find of the Chief were his lip-plates.
After this tragedy, the Muddi banned the
blowing of hunting raspberries and settled for
hunting their food on the shelves of the local
supermarket.

I am also delighted to confirm that you too
have broken yet another record. You are by
many years the World's Youngest Knight.
It gives me great pleasure to enclose your
fourteenth world-record certificate, along with
Joey's first.

Best wishes,
Eric Bibby
Keeper of the Records

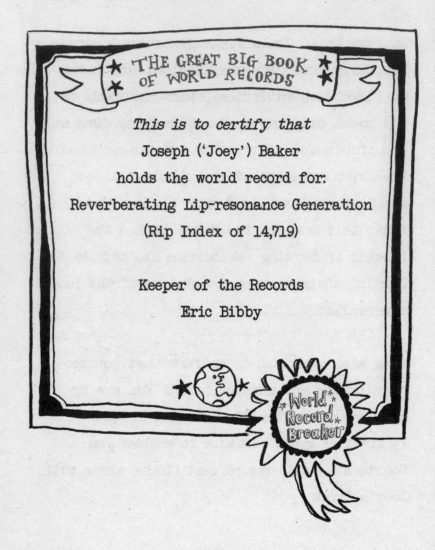

THE GREAT BIG BOOK
OF WORLD RECORDS

This is to certify that
Joseph ('Joey') Baker
holds the world record for:
Reverberating Lip-resonance Generation
(Rip Index of 14,719)

Keeper of the Records
Eric Bibby

World
Record
Breaker

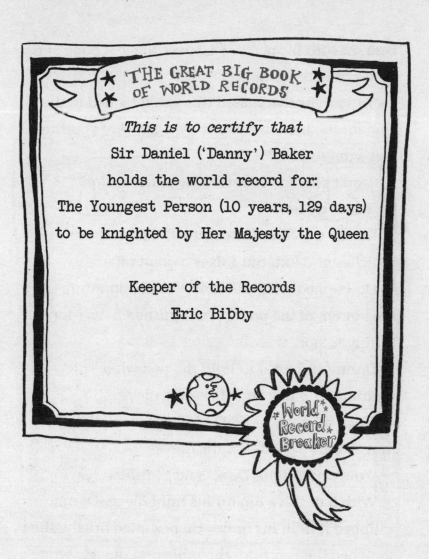

THE GREAT BIG BOOK OF WORLD RECORDS

This is to certify that
Sir Daniel ('Danny') Baker
holds the world record for:
The Youngest Person (10 years, 129 days)
to be knighted by Her Majesty the Queen

Keeper of the Records
Eric Bibby

World Record Breaker

Dad sat with his pen poised over the last page of a long printed contract.

'As soon as I've signed this you'll be tied to the club for the next five years,' he said. 'Are you sure you want to do it?'

'Don't play for Totterton Hotspoons, Dan,' begged Matthew.

Danny stared at the contract. 'I wish it was Walchester, Matt, but this is a great offer.'

Dad sighed. 'OK.' He scribbled his signature on the bottom of the paper, then pushed it over for Danny to sign.

Danny struggled to hold the pen while still wearing his bulky Stick-like-glue gloves.

'Take them off,' said Dad. 'It's your skill that makes you so good, not the gloves.'

'Your dad's right, Dan,' said Matthew. 'Go for it!'

With a decisive tug on his right glove, Danny whipped it from his hand. He hesitated briefly, then snatched the pen from the table and quickly wrote his name at the bottom of the page.

'I *really* wish it was Walchester United, Dad,' he

said. 'You know I'd rather play for your team.'

'Then it's a good job you signed the contract, isn't it?' said Dad, turning the document over to show Danny the front page.

Danny stared at it and at first didn't believe what he was seeing. At the top was the Walchester United logo, *not* the Totterton Hotspoons' one. 'What . . . ?'

Dad grinned and held out his hand. 'Welcome to Walchester United, Sir Danny.'

'What?'

'You are now – officially – the new goalkeeper for the Walchester Wonderboys Under-14 team.'

'*What?*'

'The Boss, Fergus Alexson, was always going to sign you as soon as the junior team's goalie moved up to the seniors. Walchester United wants the best.' Dad ruffled Danny's hair. 'And that's you!'

Danny leaped to his feet, punched the air and he and Matthew danced a happy jig around the room.

'Aaaaaaaaaaaaaaaaaaaaaaaaaaaaaaaaaaaaaaace!'

'Cooooooooooooooooooooooooooooooooool!'

Danny stopped suddenly. 'Does that mean I'm going to have to stop my record breaking?'

'You'll be training most nights and playing at weekends,' replied Dad. 'I don't think you'll have much time.'

'Oh no,' said Danny. 'I love breaking records.'

'Your goalkeeping seems to be better when you've got a record on the boil,' Dad said, smiling. 'So as long as it's not something that affects your game, like hanging upside down from a lamp post dressed as a packet of plums for a month, I don't see why you should stop.'

'Ace!' said Danny.

'Cool,' agreed Matthew. 'Does this mean you're going to carry on with the Long-distance Bogey-flicking attempt?'

'Dead right!' laughed Danny, shoving his finger up his nose. 'Let's get flicking!'

THE WORLD'S BIGGEST BOGEY

STEVE HARTLEY

TO THE MANAGER
The Great Big Book
of World Records
London

Dear Sir,
I have been collecting
bogeys from my nose for the
last two years.
I have stuck them all together
to make one enormous bogey. It
measures 5.3 cm in diameter and
weighs 3.6 grams. Is this a record?

Yours faithfully,

Danny Baker

(Aged nine and a bit)

WARNING
THIS STORY
MAY CONTAIN
SILLINESS

Join Danny as he attempts to smash a
load of revolting records, including:

LOUDEST TRUMP!
CHEESIEST FEET!
NITTIEST SCALP!

OUT NOW!

DANNY BAKER RECORD BREAKER

THE WORLD'S
AWESOMEST AIR-BARF

STEVE HARTLEY

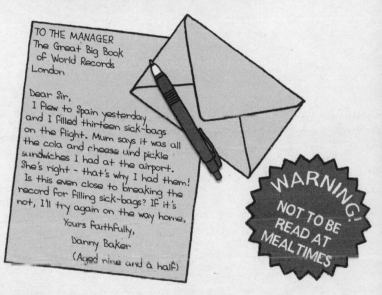

TO THE MANAGER
The Great Big Book
of World Records
London

Dear Sir,
 I flew to Spain yesterday
and I filled thirteen sick-bags
on the flight. Mum says it was all
the cola and cheese and pickle
sundwiches I had at the airport.
She's right - that's why I had them!
Is this even close to breaking the
record for filling sick-bags? If it's
not, I'll try again on the way home.
 Yours faithfully,
 Danny Baker
 (Aged nine and a half)

WARNING!
NOT TO BE
READ AT
MEALTIMES

Join Danny as he attempts to smash a
load of hilarious records, including:

FRECKLIEST FACE!
PONGIEST POTION!
SQUELCHIEST COWPATS!

OUT NOW!

THE WORLD'S
LOUDEST ARMPIT FART

STEVE HARTLEY

TO THE MANAGER
The Great Big Book
of World Records
London

Dear Sir,
Yesterday I attempted
the Continuous Musical Armpit-
farting record. I managed to play
2081 verses of 'Old MacDonald Had a
Farm' before I squeezed too hard
and bruised my fingers.
My sister was upstairs, trying to listen
to her favourite boy band. Even with
the volume turned right up she could
still hear my armpit farts! Could they
have been the Loudest Ever?
　　　Yours faithfully,
　　　Danny Baker
　(Aged nine and three quarters)

WARNING! COVER YOUR EARS!

Join Danny as he attempts to smash a
load of crazy records, including:

MESSIEST JELLY FIGHT!
CRINKLIEST WRINKLES!
VILEST VERRUCAS!

OUT NOW!